Mommy, Can You Stop the Rain?

By Rona Milch Novick, PhD

Illustrated by Anna Kubaszewska

APPLES & HONEY PRESS

To my parents, who taught me the blessing of family; to Mickey, who built one with me; to
Eitan, Yonah, and Gaby, who gave me the greatest job I'll ever have; and to Gabby, Michal, and Sarina,
who expanded my mothering horizons to include daughters and the next generation.
—RN

To my Mom. Thank you for everything.
—AK

Apples & Honey Press
An imprint of Behrman House
Millburn, New Jersey 07041
www.applesandhoneypress.com

Text copyright © 2020 by Rona Novick
Illustrations copyright © 2020 by Behrman House

ISBN 978-1-68115-555-5

Library of Congress Cataloging-in-Publication Data
Names: Novick, Rona Milch, author. | Kubaszewska, Anna, illustrator.
Title: Mommy, Can you stop the rain? / by Rona Milch Novick, PhD ; Illustrated by
   Anna Kubaszewska.
Description: Millburn, New Jersey : Apples & Honey Press, [2020] | Summary:
   Parents comfort and reassure their young daughter who, frightened by a
   storm, asks if they can stop the rain, thunder, lightning, and wind.
   Includes note to parents.
Identifiers: LCCN 2018061503 | ISBN 9781681155555 (alk. paper)
Subjects: | CYAC: Parent and child—Fiction. | Thunderstorms—Fiction. |
   Jews—Fiction.
Classification: LCC PZ7.1.N685 Can 2020 | DDC [E]—dc23
LC record available at https://lccn.loc.gov/2018061503

The illustrations in this book were created using digital techniques.

Design by Anne Redmond
Edited and art directed by Ann D. Koffsky
Printed in China

9 8 7 6 5 4 3 2 1

042125K1/B1627/A2

Mommy, can you stop the rain?

No, I cannot stop the rain.
But I will dry your hair,
and wrap you in a towel
warm from the dryer,
then we will eat iced cookies
with pink sprinkles on top.

Daddy, can you shush
the thunder?

No, I cannot shush the thunder.
But I can turn Zayde's chicken soup pot
into a drum,
and we can march around the table
like a band in a parade.

Mommy, can you turn off
the lightning?

No, I cannot turn off the lightning.
But I can shine my flashlight
into the dark corners,
and make shadow animals
climb into the Noah's ark picture on your wall.

Daddy, can you quiet the wind?

No, I cannot quiet the wind.
But I will fasten the windows tight
and rock with you under Bubbe's blanket,
and sing softly in your ear
until the wind sounds like a whisper.

Mommy and Daddy, can you send away the storm?

No, we cannot send away the storm,
   or quiet the wind,
   or turn off the lightning,
   or shush the thunder,
   or stop the rain.

But we can stay close,
and keep you cozy and warm
until the last raindrop falls . . .

. . . and the morning sun shines on you again.

When children are scared, they naturally ask parents and other grown-ups for help. And as much as the grown-ups might want to, sometimes they just can't make the scary things go away.

The parents in this story can't stop the lightning, but they can make their little girl feel better by reminding her she is not alone. They can't quiet the thunder, but they can drown it out and help her forget the sounds by banging on pots and being silly.

And rain or shine, grown-ups can always offer children comfort, reassurance, and love. It's profoundly important for children to know that they can always count on the love and care of the grown-ups in their lives.

There are even Jewish blessings, expressions of gratitude, that can be said when hearing thunder and seeing lightning during a storm. For thunder, the blessing acknowledges the Divine's "strength and power that fills the world." For lightning, one recognizes the force that "makes the works of Creation." While forces of nature may be scary to children and adults alike, Judaism recognizes that they are integral, wondrous parts of our world.

When children hear this message, they learn that someday the storms and scary times will end, and they will be okay. In this way, parents' caring comfort builds strong, healthy, independent children, who will one day manage the daily storms of life all by themselves.

With warm wishes,

Rona